Tales under the Baobab Tree

— Better Together —

Cela and Ronnie Rootz

Tales Under The Baobab Tree
- Better Together -

1st Edition

Illustrator: George Nyiko Sky
Layout designer: Jessica Colley
Editor: Su-Mia Hoffmann

Prepared for print by Preflight Books, a division of BK Publishing (Pty) Ltd
www.preflightbooks.co.za

ISBN - 13
978-0-620-94283-6

To children and families around the world.

Part of the royalties from the sale of this book will be donated to help children,
families and communities in Southern Africa build sustainable initiatives and
help realise their God-given potential.

The bolded words are in the Shona language of Zimbabwe.

"Oh wow!" Hannah exclaimed. She was amazed by all the different people sitting around the evening bonfire. The African sky was filled with bright stars and the smell of smoke hung in the air. Almost every race, colour, and culture was represented. It was exciting because this was her first bonfire in her new land.

It was a beautiful, warm night and the whole Roots family was sitting on **maponde** ('mats') under the enormous baobab tree, enjoying grilled maize cobs and roasted peanuts from the big bumper harvest.

"It was not always like this," grandfather Roots said. "Let me tell you a **ngano** ('tale')..."

"**Paivapo makare kare** ('Once upon a time, a long time ago'), in a land called **Mwene we Mutapa** ('King of the Land') there lived a beautiful biracial girl born of a **Kanata** (Canadian) mother and a Mwene we Mutapa father. Her name was **Sahara** ('dawn'). She lived with her parents **Runako** ('beautiful') and **Mhukahuru** ('big beast').

Sahara loved to smile and always carried her big smile and a very small hoe with her wherever she went. She loved to talk to people and encourage them in their time of distress. She also loved to join people in their time of laughter and joy."

"Mwene we Mutapa was well known as the 'breadbasket' of the world. This means they grew a lot of food and there was no suffering in the land. Mwene we Mutapa was a rich land because they were able to grow almost any type of food.

They grew delicious fruits like pineapples and peaches, and there were a lot of minerals like gold and diamonds hiding in the beautifully wooded mountains. Many people travelled from far and wide to find greener pastures in this land.

The king of Mwene we Mutapa, **Mambo Mugozonyatsotitsanangurirawozve** ('King Explain it in Detail'), ruled the land well…"

"...until he started keeping most of the wealth for himself, his family and close friends. The land became poor and soon nothing wanted to grow. The villages started to experience hunger. Many people lost their jobs and found it difficult to take care of their families.

The land that was once known for her wealth was now known for violence against her own people, **nzara** ('hunger') and corruption. People began to complain and some even died of starvation. There was no medicine in **zvipatara** ('hospitals') and there was no food in the silos. The king's **masoja** ('soldiers') looted from the people and beat them up."

"Why was he allowed to do that?" wondered Hannah.

"Now, Sahara was an encourager. She might have been young, but instead of joining others and complaining and doing nothing, she thought, 'I should go around the land and encourage my people'.

And so began her journey. She travelled around the land cheering people up and encouraging families and communities. She inspired them to do something using their own hands, so that they could try and rebuild their land. If there was ever someone working in their garden or community farm as she passed by, she would take her small hoe and help them.

What she was doing – taking her smile, encouragement, and small hoe around the land, helping people in their farms – become known as **Chabadza**. **Chabadza** is a Mwene we Mutapa word which symbolizes 'working together for the greater good'. If a family is working in the fields, you go with your **badza** ('hoe') and lend a hand," grandfather Roots explained.

"The people admired Sahara so much because of her hard work and sweetness that they started looking up to her and doing what she was doing. In no time, she became very popular. People talked about what Sahara was doing and they started to chant her name. Some even put her **mufananidzo** ('picture') on the street poles. They organized group gatherings to discuss how they could change their own situation. All this happened without Sahara knowing about it."

"The **mambo** ('king') was not happy with what was happening in his land. Some people who were chanting Sahara's name were arrested and put in **jeri** ('jail'). He thought Sahara was trying to take over Mwene we Mutapa because the people loved her. But they loved her because they were encouraged by her, and they had hope that one day their land would become great again."

"Finally, the king summoned Sahara to the Palace. He was very angry with her, even though the people were very happy with her. 'You want to take over my kingdom, you – **you child**.' The king spoke very harshly to her. 'You are turning my people against me,' he added.

'No, no, no, my king,' Sahara said, kneeling before Mambo Mugozonyatsotitsanangurirawozve.

'I have seen our people suffering and dying because of hunger. Instead of complaining, I thought I should go around the land encouraging our people. I help them use their hands and be productive. I know, my king, you are very busy looking for ways you can return our land to its glory days and become the breadbasket of the world once again. I am trying to help my king. And our land.' She looked at the king with her big, brown, smiling eyes with a grin that almost touched her ears."

"There was nothing the king could do after that big smile. The king smiled back and commanded that all the hidden silos be opened and food be distributed to the people! He ordered all the minerals that he was keeping for himself be sold and the money used to develop the land!

The king announced that Sahara was the new King's Representative of the land. She would organize people who would go around the land to search for ways to develop communities."

"In just a few years, the land of Mwene we Mutapa was back to its glory days and it was the breadbasket and jewel of the world once again. The king took Sahara to the side and whispered to her, 'You have such a gentle spirit within you, who is that spirit that lives inside you? I want it. Is it the spirit of our ancestors? Who is it?'

Sahara humbly and quietly answered the king, 'The spirit you see in me is not the one you mention. It is the King of kings, the Lord of lords, the conquering Lion of the tribe of Judah. And of Mwene we Mutapa. Jesus Christ! Do you – ?'

Before she could finish, the king shouted, 'Yes, please! I need Him.'"

"The king was a much happier man now and he ordered that the name of the land be changed to **Ubuntu** ('oneness') and that everyone was to pray to the God of Sahara. The people, too, were happy and excited and they shouted, 'Long live the king!'. The land of Ubuntu continued producing good crops and providing work for its people. Everyone was united, and transformation could be seen across the land."

"And so," **sekuru** ('grandfather') Roots quietly added, "it was because of a young girl, using only a smile and a hoe – and the name of Jesus – that the king was changed, and the land was brought together once again. That is why you see so many people of all walks of life enjoying the land together, spending time together, and loving each other. And for that, we will never be the same!"

Hannah was deeply touched by this miraculous story of transformation, not only of a man, but of a nation. She sat back, looked up at the millions of twinkling stars in the dark sky, and with the evening buzz of cicadas in the distance, she smiled to herself. As her eyes filled with tears, she whispered to herself, "What an amazing place to be!"

Discussion questions:

What if Sahara didn't plant a seed? Would the story be the same?

What was the seed?

How was it planted?

How would you have reacted if you were Sahara? If you were the king?

What does the Bible teach about working together?

Is spiritual food more important than physical food?

Can you plant a seed where you are?

What are different ways that people might be suffering around you?

What tools do you have to make a difference?

In what ways can you and your family bring change? Help others?

In what ways can we unite, or bring, people together?

Do these Bible verses resonate with you? If yes, what are they saying to you?

Write down five or more prayer requests that you can pray for every day.

Do you find it difficult to pray for your enemies? What does the Word of God say about that?

Study Verses: How do these verses relate to the story?

"I urge, then, first of all, that petitions, prayers, intercession and thanksgiving be made for all people- for kings and all those in authority, that we may live peaceful and quiet lives in all godliness and holiness."

— 1 Timothy 2:1-2

"Fear not for I have redeemed you, I have summoned you by name, you are Mine."

— Isaiah 43:1

"Speak up for those who cannot speak for themselves, for the rights of all who are destitute."

— Proverbs 31:8

"Even so the body is not made up of one part but of many."

— 1 Corinthians 12:14

"Two are better than one, because they have a good return for their labour: If either of them falls down, one can help the other up..."

— Ecclesiastes 4:9-10a

"Humble yourselves before the Lord, and He will lift you up."

— James 4:10

"...if my people, who are called by my name, will humble themselves and pray and seek my face and turn from their wicked ways, then I will hear from heaven, and I will forgive their sins and will heal their land."

— 2 Chronicles 7:14

"He guides the humble in what is right and teaches them His way."

— Psalm 25:9

Use your knowledge from the story to complete the crossword.

Down:

1. What is Hannah's family name?
The _____ family.

2. What is Sahara's eye colour? _____

3. What does sekuru translate to in English?
_____

4. "The African sky was filled with bright
_____ "

5. As her eyes filled with tears, she whispered to herself,
"What an _____ place to be!"

6. "The king was a much happier man now and he ordered that the name of the land be changed to
_____ ('oneness')"

Across:

7. What was the King's name?
_____ Mugozonyatsotitsanangurirawozve

8. Mwene we Mutapa was well known as the
'_____' of the world.

9. What does Sahara translate to in English?
_____

10. What was the name of the land before the King renamed it at the end of the story?
_____

Words to find:

AFRICA

WORLD

KING

SKY

TOGETHER

WORK

SAHARA

FAMILY

TREE

FIRE

Q	U	V	Z	A	S	J	F	H	X	W	T	F	Q	S
Y	S	K	Y	W	C	Z	D	F	G	Y	O	B	A	Z
B	B	A	T	K	D	F	I	R	E	V	G	B	R	E
N	R	M	A	K	H	J	H	O	I	Z	E	X	M	Y
V	A	F	R	I	C	A	Y	R	G	V	T	R	E	E
E	N	D	T	N	P	G	E	O	B	L	H	U	Y	D
Q	C	W	I	G	X	G	I	L	U	U	E	M	Z	L
M	R	O	Y	L	W	V	B	P	W	O	R	K	K	B
U	O	R	S	S	S	A	H	A	R	A	L	J	D	C
X	W	L	P	Q	W	F	K	D	T	I	Y	L	G	J
E	Z	D	A	F	A	M	I	L	Y	F	T	Z	S	K
D	B	W	S	V	A	X	T	O	W	E	T	T	D	Z

Help Hannah Find Her Way Home

Colour the image of Sahara and the King

Draw your own village: